Cowgirl Kate and Cocoa

Partners

Cowgirl Kate and Cocoa

Partners

Written by **Erica Silverman**

Painted by **Betsy Lewin**

Harcourt, Inc.

Orlando   Austin   New York   San Diego   Toronto   London

To Elina Gordyenko, a wonderful
reader and rider—E. S.

With thanks to Patty Peoples Smith
for providing the locale—B. L.

Text copyright © 2006 by Erica Silverman
Illustrations copyright © 2006 by Betsy Lewin

www.HarcourtBooks.com

First Harcourt paperback edition 2007

Library of Congress Cataloging-in-Publication Data
Silverman, Erica.
Cowgirl Kate and Cocoa: partners/written by Erica Silverman; painted by Betsy Lewin.
p. cm.
Summary: Cocoa the horse herds the cows with Cowgirl Kate, helps her practice her roping skills,
and wishes he could wear boots instead of horseshoes.
[1. Cowgirls—Fiction. 2. Horses—Fiction. 3. Cows—Fiction.]
I. Lewin, Betsy, ill. II. Title.
PZ7.S58625Co 2006
[E]—dc22   2004027435
ISBN 978-0-15-202125-2
ISBN 978-0-15-206010-7 (pb)

H G F E D C B A
H G F E D   (pb)

Printed in Singapore

The illustrations in this book were done in watercolors on
Strathmore one-ply Bristol paper.
The display type was hand lettered by Georgia Deaver.
The text type was set in Filosofia Regular.
Color separations by Bright Arts Ltd., Hong Kong
Printed and bound by Tien Wah Press, Singapore
Production supervision by Christine Witnik
Designed by Scott Piehl

Chapter 1
New Shoes

"Cocoa," said Cowgirl Kate,
"this man has come
   to give you new horseshoes."

Cocoa glared at the man.

Then he turned and trotted away.

Cowgirl Kate ran after him.

"What's the matter?" she asked.

Cocoa snorted.

"I don't want horseshoes," he said.

"I want cowboy boots."

"But Cocoa," said Cowgirl Kate,
"you are a horse."

Cocoa snorted again.

"I am a cowhorse," he said,

"and I want cowboy boots, just like yours."

"But they won't fit you," she replied.

"Let me try one," he said.

Cowgirl Kate took off a boot.

She held it for Cocoa.

Cocoa lifted one hoof.

He pushed and pushed,

but he could not get his hoof into the boot.

"I'm sorry," said Cowgirl Kate,

"but cowboy boots only fit people."

Cocoa's head drooped.

"People are lucky," he said.

"Lucky?" asked Cowgirl Kate.

She pointed.

"Cocoa, what do you see on the barn?"

"A horseshoe," said Cocoa.

"And what do you see
on the house?" she asked.
"A horseshoe," he said.
She led him down the road.
"What do you see on the fence?"
"*Another* horseshoe," he said.

"Cocoa," she asked, "do you know why
  people hang horseshoes everywhere?"
"Of course," said Cocoa,
"because nobody wants to wear them."
  Cowgirl Kate shook her head.

"No," she said.
"It's because they believe
  horseshoes bring good luck."
"Good luck?" asked Cocoa.
"I want good luck."
  He galloped back to the barn.

He stood still while the man
put on his new shoes.

Then he trotted outside.

"I am lucky!" he cried.

"I have lucky horseshoes!"

He bumped Cowgirl Kate with his head.

"And you are lucky, too," he said.

"You are lucky because you have me."

Chapter 2
Hide-and-Seek

"Let's play hide-and-seek," said Cocoa.

"Not now," said Cowgirl Kate.

"Now we have to count the calves."

So Cowgirl Kate and Cocoa counted the calves.
"Molly's calf is missing," said Cowgirl Kate.
"Maybe he's playing hide-and-seek," said Cocoa.

"He could be hurt," said Cowgirl Kate.
"We have to find him!"
So Cowgirl Kate and Cocoa
looked for Molly's calf.
They looked in the bushes.

They looked in the gully.

They looked in the tall grass.
"There he is!" cried Cocoa.

Cocoa pushed.

Cowgirl Kate pulled.

And together they took the calf back to Molly.

Molly mooed and nuzzled her calf.

"Good work, partner," said Cowgirl Kate.

Cocoa nudged her.

"Now can we play hide-and-seek?"
he asked.

"Yes," said Cowgirl Kate.

"Yippee!" said Cocoa. "You hide,
and I'll count to twenty."
He closed his eyes.

"One, two, three . . . ," he began.

"Count slowly," said Cowgirl Kate.

"Four . . . five . . . ," he continued.
Cowgirl Kate tiptoed away.

She hid behind a big tree.
She waited for Cocoa to find her.
She waited ...
and waited.
What's taking him so long?
she wondered.

She peeked out.
I don't see Cocoa anywhere,
but I do see his hoofprints.

She followed them all the way to the cornfield.

Cocoa was munching a mouthful of corn.

"What happened to hide-and-seek?"
cried Cowgirl Kate.

Cocoa grinned.

"My new game is even better,"
he said.

"It's called . . .
hide-and-*eat*."

Chapter 3
Roping

Cowgirl Kate stared at the fence post.
She twirled her rope.
Whoosh.
"You missed," said Cocoa.

Whoosh.

"You missed again," said Cocoa.

"Horseflies!" Cowgirl Kate grumbled.

She stared hard at the fence post.
She twirled her rope.
Whoosh.
"Yeehaw!" cried Cowgirl Kate.
"I roped the fence post."

Whoosh.

"I roped the mailbox."

Whoosh.

"I roped the ladder."

Cowgirl Kate walked all around.
"What else can I rope?" she asked.
"How about a cow?" Cocoa suggested.
"Mom says I'm not ready to rope a real cow,"
   said Cowgirl Kate.

"But . . ."

She smiled.

"We can pretend *you* are a cow."

Cocoa snorted.

"I am much too smart to be a cow...
    even a pretend cow," he said.

"I'll give you an apple," said Cowgirl Kate.

"I'd rather have pizza," said Cocoa.

"Then I'll give you pizza," she said.

"Okay," he said. "I'll be a cow.
  But I will not say moo."

Cowgirl Kate twirled her rope.

Whoosh.

"You missed," said Cocoa.

Whoosh.

"You missed again," said Cocoa.

"Horseflies!" said Cowgirl Kate.

Cocoa pranced this way and that.

"You'll never catch me!"
he called.

Cowgirl Kate pointed.

"Look, Cocoa," she called,

"timothy grass!"

Cocoa swung his head around to look.

Cowgirl Kate twirled her rope.

Whoosh.

"I got you!" she cried.

"You tricked me," Cocoa said.

His head drooped.

"I'm not so smart after all."

"You are very smart," said Cowgirl Kate.

"You just can't resist timothy grass."

"Timothy grass!" cried Cocoa.

   And he galloped off.

"Come back with my rope!" Cowgirl Kate called.

"Moooooo," Cocoa called back.

"Pretend I'm a cow.

   Come and get me!"

Chapter 4
Partners

"Hurry, Cocoa," said Cowgirl Kate.
"We have to check the cows."
"I'm too hot," said Cocoa.
"Check the cows without me."
"We are partners through hot and cold,"
  said Cowgirl Kate,
"and partners do everything together."
  So Cowgirl Kate and Cocoa checked the cows.

"Those cows sure look hot," said Cocoa.

"They sure do," said Cowgirl Kate.

"Let's move them under the trees."

"I'm too weak," said Cocoa.

"Move them under the trees without me."

"We are partners through weak and strong,"
    said Cowgirl Kate,

"and partners do everything together."

So Cowgirl Kate and Cocoa nudged the cows.
They pushed and prodded until one cow moved,
and another followed, and then another.
Finally, all the cows were standing
in the shade of the trees.
"Look!" cried Cocoa.
"There goes Molly's calf."

Cowgirl Kate and Cocoa
chased him around and around.
When they ran to the right,
the calf ran to the left.

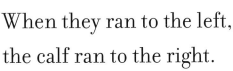

When they ran to the left,
the calf ran to the right.

"*MOOO!*" Molly bellowed. "*MOOO!*"
  The calf stood still.
  His ears perked up.
  His tail twitched.
"Look!" cried Cocoa.
"He's going back to Molly."
"Good work, partner!" said Cowgirl Kate.

She sighed.

"That calf sure likes to make trouble."

"He sure does," said Cocoa,

"but we are always ready for him."

Cowgirl Kate took the reins.

"We can head back now," she said.

"Not yet," said Cocoa.

"There's one more thing we have to do."

And he trotted . . .

KERSPLASH!

. . . into the river.

"*Ack!*" cried Cowgirl Kate.

"Couldn't you go swimming without me?"

Cocoa turned his head
and splashed water at her.
"We are partners through wet and dry,"
he said,
"and partners do everything together."